The House that Gaylord Built

To my mother who taught me to believe in ghosts and that talking to them was beautiful, rewarding and revealing. To my grandchildren, Joaquin, Alexia, Maxi, Leon and Vicente, in whose spirits I hope to live.

PREFACE

This story is both real and fictional

relating the relationship that existed

between a woman and a man that had

died many years ago but very much

present in the house particularly in this

one room of the house. The author was

born in a bedroom where a woman had

died in childbirth many years before.

Perhaps that was the reason that she

was inextricably involved with the souls

of the departed. But she also knew how

it felt to die and come back. At the early

age of six-months, she was afflicted with

peritonitis and was expected to die within a few hours. Her mother, who had the ability also to communicate with the dead, was told by a dead woman in the middle of the night to seek a man named Jose, riding on a horse, a peasant, whose blood would save her daughter. The mother did not hesitate and after hours of searching all over town, a rough looking man on a white horse named Jose suddenly appeared in front of the house. Coming down the horse Jose was trembling with fear. He had heard that he needed to provide some of his blood to this little girl or she would promptly die. With not a second to lose, Jose was strapped to a chair, the blue veins in his strong left arm were visible by everyone. The doctor then proceeded to insert the needle into his arm and the dark red blood started to flow into a bag next to the chair. Jose calmed down when he realized that no harm was going to come to him. He watched intently in how the doctor inserted another smaller needle into a vein in the chubby right leg of the small child. Opening the plastic tube on the bag that contained the blood of Jose allowed the blood to flow into the little veins of the child. She had lied there for many hours, not opening the eyes, breathing with great difficulty and hardly moving. Not an hour had gone by that suddenly her eyes opened and a little smile appeared on the round full face. Her mother threw herself to the floor and kneeling down started praying. This was indeed a miracle and Jose was right away pronounced the savior. This child was never to get sick again, never had a surgery or took medication but her personality changed forever from one of a quiet, peaceful child to one that was rebellious, contentious and wild. She had to be tied to a chair in order for the hair to be combed. None could cut her nails and she will use them as weapons against her brother and sister. Oftem she refused to eat to ger her way. She was the antithesis of what her mother had wished as a daughter. Only one person was allowed to touch her and groom her and that was Concha, the loving grandmother who always found positive aspects of her. Always defending her from parents and siblings Concha was convinced that this child was destined for big challenges given her energy and uncompromising personality. Just wait until she grows up, you all will be proud of her Concha would say. A tomboy, she loved to climb trees and play games against the boys finding her most precious moments in her old wooden boat where she rowed for hours getting far away from home and everyone in it. She found peace floating on the water, the smell of the sea numbed her senses, and the waves hitting against the skull of the boat calmed her mind. She did most of her thinking in that boat, she saw a world at peace, a harmony not to be found at home or in the real world, a sense of belonging to something more sublime and magic.

She lived in a middle-class family, a big house, with servants that kept everything in order. But that was the image, in reality, that home was plagued by turmoil and painful surprises.   She knew that she was not the favorite of either father or mother and that her behavior and physical appearance did nothing to endear them to both parents. Her mother claimed all the time that it was the blood of Jose that had changed that child forever. At times her mother would claim that she was not really her own child but that she was adopted to justify the lack of love she had for this one child. It was this distance created by both parents that enable her to be so independent, self-sufficient and nonconformist. She did not care what people thought of her, she knew she was born of these two beings that rejected her only to conform to social norms. She only found refuge in those adoring arms of her grandmother Concha. Concha would console her and made excuses for her parents' behavior. There was nothing wrong with her, she was different that was all. She lovingly called her "mi Prieta" my dark one, because she was darker than the other siblings. When Concha died alone. She left only one thing and one thought, a white linen handkerchief embroidered with the words "Mi Prieta" and asked that it be given to me so I will never forget her.   Only my grandmother Concha found me beautiful and smart. She will spend long hours with her, at times teaching me how to embroider, but most of the time describing vignettes from her childhood. She was born in Manzanillo, Cuba, one of the most beautiful women I have ever seen. Her waist-long hair was like those you see in the shampoo ads. She was always superbly dressed and made-up. She will never leave her room until all that was achieved and she smelled nice.

She was so poor that her house only had a latrine (outside bathroom) and could not afford make up or perfume. I had a secret operation where she will bring little empty glass bottles and I will fill them out with mother's expensive French perfume. I now know that my wellbeing is due to Concha's nurturing love. I never said good-bye to Concha, she died of a heart attack while I was in the U.S. I know she died in peace and in love. When I feel down because of life wrong turn, I called her to help me. I do this the way Concha told me, "you look at the moon and raise your right hand and call my name and say Abuela give me a hand".

Her mother always worried about her future. Who would dare marry you? she would often say. She responded to her mother often that the only thing she wanted in life was to be a mother. She had one redeeming quality, she was very smart, getting high grades in school. She strongly believed she could be anything she wanted to be if she put her mind to it. And so it was that she was successful in luring the most handsome and desirable bachelor in town, Felipe. Tall, blond and green eyes he was the choice of every single girl in that town. None knows what Felipe found attractive in her but she remained her loyal friend to the point of making it possible for her to travel to the U.S. during a moment of great panic in Cuba. She remained uncontrollably strong and healthy until one September afternoon in 2018 when she was given the worst news of a disease that would hunt her for the rest of her life. But this story will be told later.

I Never said Good-bye

It was a cloudy afternoon in this port city

in Cuba, the place where I was born and

lived happily until this day. My parents

decided that both my brother and I had

to leave Cuba. Panic had taking hold on

every good and well-intentioned parent

in Cuba. The word that went around

was that every minor child was to be

removed from their parents and send to

training camps in remote areas of the

island. Without seeking the truth, my

parents made the decision to ship us

both to Miami, where an operation

managed by the Catholic Bureau in that

City was accepting children to later be

sent to foster homes and orphanages.

The threat never materialized and not

one child was ever removed from the

loving arms of their parents. But the

damage was done.

The trip to Miami became the main concern in all homes, sort of a hysteria to save the children. At home lots of preparations were being made for this trip to Miami. Neither my brother or I had ever traveled abroad, much less without our parents. It did not fit in the scheme of a controlling mother that never allowed us to even step out of the house without an adult at our side. Mother was reconciled in the belief that this was a temporary stay, a few weeks, perhaps a month, and the regime will be deposed and both my brother and I would be back to her. To calm nerves, mother decided to make me a dress, it had a knitted collar that she herself did and the material had sparkles all over. I looked so grown up and elegant. I was 14 years old and had no say on any of this. My only wish was to see my grandmother Concha, who at this time was having heart problems and was staying with us until she felt better. My mother insisted that I did not share this trip with her as she may become agitated and anxious. I sat down in her little bed, the one where she taught me how to embroider, where she would tell me stories about her youth and her love affairs. She never spoke of the future but centered on the good times, those gone by. However, this day she was very philosophical about life and how we should live it. I now think that she knew that was going to be the last time she would see me and held me in her arms. She asked me to live in the present and reject any notion of the future and that way I will have no expectations and no disappointments. The future has yet to be written, she added. She continued as if she was reciting a phrase from a book; As human being we yearn for predictability, for stable live because it is difficult to live with unknowns, to have to adapt to an ever changing world, and yet, she said looking directly at my eyes, you must adapt if you are going to live fully without regrets or anger. With that she gave me a big embrace, looked at me once more and turned her face so I will not see her cry. Concha died one month later and I never said good-bye to her. They tell me that years later when they opened her grave, her long silver hair was intact

Arrival in Miami was chaotic at best. Two planes arrived every day each carrying 300 kids, most of them crying for their parents. At the end 14,000 children left Cuba through this program that was later called Peter Pan.

At the airport there was a priest, his name was Padre Jorge, he had a bag full of Hershey bars that he threw at each one of us. He tried very hard to cheer us up and talked about America, the land of freedom and opportunity. He never spoke about the Cuba we had left behind or when we would reunite with our parents. Maybe he knew. After 15 minutes with Padre Jorge, we were all boarded into a school bus that would take us to Florida City Military barracks. The trip took for ever and the view outside was very rural, few houses, farmers cultivating their products and nothing else. I had one big bag where I

tried to put everything I had of value,
photographs, my address book, the
handkerchief that Concha gave, and $5.
There were restrictions as to what you
could bring. No jewelry was allowed
only a wedding band that mother made
with a gold coin my father gave her the
day I was born. It is engraved inside
with my name and the day of my birth. I
still wear it to this day that ring has
never left my finger.

The barracks were distributed in two
floor buildings, each building had a
couple that was in charge of cleaning
and providing food for us. Mine was a

Mexican couple that had two children one of them one year old. They were very strict with us and I was separated from my brother because in the barracks only small children and girls were accepted. I felt very lonely and was not able to visit him except once a month.

As I had graduated from high school and was fluent in English, I was asked to teach the smaller children English. It kept me busy and out of trouble. I lost notion of how long I was there but with each day I became more restless and anxious. I remember my grandmother words when I left that I needed to adapt.

I never went back to Cuba and I never said good=by to mt beautiful Cuba. My parents were allowed to leave the island four years later and my bother and I reunited with them. I am not sure I would put my children through a similar ordeal. While the experience taught to be strong, determined and self-reliant it came at a very high price.

Gaylord's House

On a cloudy September afternoon in

Miami Beach the family stopped at a

grey house that seemed abandoned.

The grass grown, windows and doors

missing, peeling paint, darkness inside.

But there was a certain charm or

perhaps a simple attraction for being so

different from the rest of the houses.

Although late driving to a friends' house

the family turned around and stopped in

the front of the house. For a while I

stood silent, inspecting the majestic

front of the house, the wooden door

laced with brass, the balcony that

presided the house, the elegant parapet that culminated the front tower. The house transmitted a feeling of loneliness and pride of once being the jewel of this neighborhood. I hesitated to come in although there were no doors on the side of the house and there were windows missing from the front. However, I felt a strong pull, as if someone inside was inviting me to come in and discover a secret that had been buried for so many years.

At first sight all I could see were broken doors and windows, mattresses all over the floor, a smell of abandonment.

Obviously, some homeless individuals found the huge living room a perfect place to spend the night. The door leading to the courtyard was missing and the wooden floor in front of it was wet and rotten. The ceilings, doors, windows and staircase were all painted with a dark brown oil paint. Beneath layers of paint lied the beautiful Dade County pine. I realized the enormous work that it will be to bring back that beautiful house back to its glorious days. Despite the years of neglect. I was surprised that the main features of house had remained pristine and untouched. None had bothered to upgrade the kitchen or bathrooms as the house remained as when first built back in 1926. Some of the windows and doors were damaged by water sipping through the ceiling or simply because they did not close anymore and were exposed to the outside. In the kitchen nothing worked. There was no fridge or stove only an old sink that was no longer connected to the plumbing. There was a bathroom between the living room and the kitchen and the area leading to the courtyard had retained the French door and only some of the glass was missing.

Upstairs the master bedroom had

remained almost intact. All the closets

were lined with beautiful mahogany and

the balcony unto the living room was

intact, only the door leading to the

balcony was missing.   To the right of

the room were two French doors,

painted white and like the day there

were placed there. The doors led to a

brightly lighted room.   When I entered

the room I had the feeling that I was not

alone and that someone was watching

every move I was making.   The window

facing east was opened and you can

smell the ocean salt from there. There

was no furniture only an old mattress

where some homeless person had slept in. I kept coming back to this room, looking for somebody, something that I needed to know. Surrounded by windows and covered with a beautiful oak ceiling it once was an open terrace from where the ocean could be seen back when the house was the only structure standing up in the entire neighborhood. The window facing the ocean, like the rest of the windows in that room, had a brass mechanism to open and close by rotating a leaver. It was hard to close because the window had been exposed to the outside and did not fit together anymore. When I tried to close it by bringing the two sides together, a strong wind pushed it back open. To this day that window cannot be closed and a gentle sea breeze bathes that room constantly. Someone had painted that room bright green and when you scratch some of the paint you found that originally it was painted light blue, a color that was used at that time to paint walls. When I left the room I heard a noise that made me look back. It was coming from the open window facing the ocean.

Some strange force pulled me back to the room and without realizing it I was in the green room and the window blew

open. It was a cool windy April night

and I was so tired that I did not even

looked up. When I did, after a few

minutes, I saw this cloud in front of the

window. I wiped my tears in disbelief,

and then I saw these black trimmed

glasses. I focused my eyes again and I

could clearly see this round face man,

with white bushy hair smiling at me. I

just did not know what to do, stay or run,

I remember my mother and her wise

words about how to deal with the

unknown. I did not know his name nor

did he introduce himself. He just started

talking to me in a soft sweat voice.

Surprisingly he was aware of all that had happened to me since we had moved. Later I always saw him in the midst of a fog, but I heard his voice loud and clear, stronger every time and his dark black trimmed glasses what the first indication that he was there.   After a few minutes the vision stopped and I again continued my journey through this mysterious house.

Walking towards the end of the second floor she was surprised to see the entire balcony overseeing the court yard covered with plywood. Apparently, water had started to sip through and the owners just covered the entire balcony.

One of the first things I did was to tear

those wooden planks to find that the

balcony was there, in all its splendor,

with complete ceiling and French doors

leading to the bedrooms. What a nice

surprise. There were three bathrooms,

the last one was all lavender and did not

work. The last room had a lot of water

damage and the ceiling was about to

collapse. Yet there it was, the house

had withstood years of neglect and

misuse, as if waiting for someone to

discover it and bring it back to life.

The size of the house and the level of disrepair made me pause. Where do you begin? Making the house function again, new electrical system, replacing all the plumbing, roof, replacing doors and windows where there was none. I do not believe anyone would come to the house but security became an issue with me. Only one electrical socket worked, in the room next to the master bedroom of course, and at night the entire family would gather in that room to eat, talk and sleep   I cooked on a small electrical plate and wash dishes on the sidewalk as there was no running water inside the house.   I almost was glad that I had to endure such situation because It bought the family together, we had never talked so much before or share so much. In fact, I looked back at those days with joy. I always wanted a close family and I had it then and yet I did not realize that until years later. There was a magnetic force in that house, pulling us together so we would stay.

I had been living in the house for a week when a car from the City Office of Code Enforcement arrived. Apparently, some neighbors had complained I washing dishes on the sidewalk. A big fat man smoking a cigar just pushed the front

door open and walked in. No greetings,

just a command we are condemning this

house and you must leave it by 5:00

p.m. this afternoon. I asked him who

he was and he never showed me any

credentials, just pushed me aside and

repeated the summon—out of this

house by 5:00 p.m and then he placed a

sign on the door "CONDENMED". The

family did not have a place to go, and

that was our home. We decided that we

were not going anywhere. I would only

come back after dark and on week-

ends, when City staff was not around.

They came back the next day and the

next day but gave up after a week of not finding anyone around.

The house had been for sale for over five years. The owner decided to put it for auction when I started asking the owner as to the purchase price for the house, he told me that he already had done the arrangements for auction. The auction took place in a hotel in Miami Beach. The large room was crowded with people. Several hotels were being auctioned at ridiculous prices. When the house came up only two bidders were interested, I and middle-aged man who looked like a developer. When the bid of $100,000 was reached, the other bidder stopped and the house was purchased for $100,000. The excitement of the bidding stopped when I went back to the house and saw what was purchased—a derelict. I   got to know the other bidder better as he came years later to see what had done with the house. He too was driven to this house because of some ethical mandate, he had promised to himself to repair it, bring it back to its glory days. He told me that he had found the original plans of the house and brought them to us the next day. Something of a miracle he said, and then he told us about the man that built it—John Gaylord, a crazy guy; rich railroad entrepreneur from Cleveland, Ohio, who once visited Santa Fe and felt in love with the "adobe" houses. He brought architects from all over the Southwest so that the house was to be built true to the standards and the style. He spared no money in the design and construction. The house became his most precious possession. Every winter he would come from Cleveland with the entire family and the house would glimmer with laughter, lights and party goers. Who would have guessed looking at the house today. If Gaylord could see what his beautiful Santa Fe house had become he would cry endlessly. I too felt a sense of lost and disgrace. John Gaylord was born 1998 in Cleveland, Ohio, the 11th child of a middle-class family. He raised a fortune in the railroad/ business and had only one child a daughter that had died of cancer at a young age. Gaylord had endured the hardship of the II World War, survived the Big Depression of 1926 but more interesting the Third Pandemic of the year 1855. Originating in the province of Yunnam, China, claiming 15 million lives around the world as infected rats, travelling in steamship, made it all the way to San Francisco and the rest of the world. Ending in 1950, it achieved several breakthroughs and a better understanding by doctors of the bubonic plague. A Chinese Doctor Alexander Yestin identified the bacillus that was later called Yersinian vaccine. My admiration for Gaylord grew after knowing what he had endured and the beauty he created during those troubling and uncertain times—his house. I learned that day, that I would restore that house as tribute to this man that had overcome so much and dreamed so high. I felt secure in myself that if he was watching, he would be smiling and grateful.

As I stood in the middle of the living room, I was smiling and in owe. Looking at the house in a different way, as if it had just been built and enchanted with the knowledge now that I could bring it back. Luckily, the house has not been defaced and remains in a pristine condition thanks to the way it remained abandoned and beyond repair. I could see that but how long and how much it would be before I had a normal house to live in.

Getting repairs done took a while, because of lack of funds and also finding the right people, someone that will not rip things off, respect the nature of the house, follow our strict instructions as to what to leave intact and the price. I never thought of how expensive it would become the fixing of the house instead of building a new one. The entire family would work on what they could, restoring, repainting the walls, doors and windows. Taking off layers of paints became a long and hard job. Finally, a sand blaster did the job and that created so much dust that I had to sleep outside.

A sort of miracle, or perhaps

orchestrated by someone. happened

that summer called Andrew. The

deadliest hurricane in history that

destroyed and killed more than 50

people went through the area. When it

was over only parts of the old roof flew

and some window glass broke. Water

had come in through the roof making the

inside of the house even worst. Most of

the furniture was damaged.   We

decided to call the insurance agent and

he came paper and pencil in hand. He

thoroughly inspected the house;

sometimes quietly asking himself why

such a lovely family would want to live in

a place like this. I think he felt sorry for all of us.   He looked with pity at the wet floors, no electricity or plumbing and now, without a roof. After a few hours he left with a mountain of notes. This house was built days before another catastrophic hurricane back in 2026 that killed thousands in the area of South Beach. I was told that nothing happened to the house then only minor window breaks as the house was built on the premise that hurricanes will knock on its doors. To our surprise the insurance approved a total of $87,000 in damages and issued a check two weeks later. I still remember the day the check arrived, I stood again in the middle of

the living room in amazement and joy.

Now the house can be fixed the

plumbing and have electricity. The

journey back to 1926 started that day.

Was Gaylord involved in this miracle?

Half Medium

I was born in an old Victorian house in Cuba called the San Carlos house. Big foyer and sitting room followed by a row of bedrooms each facing a big courtyard. At the end an old kitchen, wood stove and a fridge that required ice to keep cold. As a child I would wait for the ice man to come in every week, carrying a big chuck of ice on his back where he had placed a piece of jute to keep himself dry. A few feet away from the kitchen he will pull the ice with the jute, place it on the tile floor and push it all the way to the front of the fridge. He never ever missed. As children we entertained ourselves with this type of activities, we did not have expensive toys, only ourselves, my seven cousins, my sister Loly and the only boy in the family my brother Roberto. How innocent and happy we were and how much harmony there was in that house. That was what I hoped to replicate in Gaylord's house, big enough to house all of my children in private bedrooms and bathrooms and with a courtyard where the family and children would get together. That was my dream and my hope. It never happened.

Dolores, my mother, gave birth to this baby with an enormous head and big eyes on the 4th of July, 1945 in the second bedroom of this San Carlos house, both parents were expecting a boy, having had a girl 12 months earlier. A boy like my brother Roberto, who came three years later, blue eye, white skin and blonde hair. Instead they got me and for many years they joked that they had found me in a garbage can abandoned. Skinny, very dark, and with hair always undone, they expected very little of me, they worried if someone one day would marry me. Mother will tell us the story of the woman that had died of

childbirth in the same room I was born.
She said she spoke to her often and she
was unable to die in peace. In fact,
Mother was considered a half-medium
by most voodoos for her ability to see
and talk to dead people. She repeated
the story often of the woman that had
died of childbirth where I was born. She
would appear without a head in the
middle of the night and cried to mother
about her unfortunate death that
prevented her for becoming a mother to
her only child. Another recurrent story
was that of Don Manuel, the patriarch of
the family and owner of the house who
hanged himself in the foyer wearing his

blue stripped pajamas. Mother had rushed from her bed when a knock on the front door in the middle of the night. She never got to the door, instead she pumped into Manuel, who was hanging happily on the foyer iron door, and there sitting down and eight- month pregnant, she was able to visualized the old man. Everyone in the house was horrified with the story but were able to identify the corpse as that of Don Manuel. Mother will always corroborate with others what she had seen and inevitably they will concur with her that she had in fact seen and talked to a dead person.   Mother was very proud of this gift she had because she felt she was helping those

who had died and were restless.

Concha's most vital undertaking was to

teach me how to deal with father

Roberto. My father, a tall, handsome

and highly educated man, suffered from

schizophrenia and resorting to drinking

to make it through the day. A good

loving man, that had a successful

business, studied abroad and was able

to speak three languages perfectly.

Born to a well-to-do family, to a strong

and domineering mother and a weak

and sick father. Unfortunately for

Roberto and all of us his father died

when he was 2 weeks old. His mother always wanted to have a daughter and so, deprived of all boundaries and reprimands, she dressed her blond and blue eye child as a girl, put ribbons on the long curly hair and sent him to school that way. Unfortunately, Roberto, had been born as a well-defined heterosexual and succumbed to the cruelties of Cienfuegos society that had no qualms towards individuals who were, at that time, in the closet. Roberto had an arsenal of knifes, guns and scissors in his closet and he will pull them about when he was drunk aiming only at the one person he loved; the most, my mother. I would get in the middle of the fight, getting cuts on the arms and legs, in order to protect my mother. Roberto resented me for that, this child who is supposed to be nothing, that will never amount to anything, dares to challenge the father's authority. I was many times in danger of being killed myself. Her father, in a moment of rage, would put on fire the mosquito net over my bed, throw a hot plate of white beans, one day an old typewriter ended up inches away from me

There was no harmony present within the family not even from mother who always struggled with being accepted in society. A very pretty girl from a very poor family growing up in a small town she had gone to the big city to get an education. The moment Roberto saw this pretty girl he went crazy.   So intense was his love for her that just before he died he threatened to kill her so she would accompany him to the ever- lasting glory. We lived in fear, not knowing what the new day will bring, would father be normal that day or not. Everyone in town resented the fact that she had stolen the most desirous bachelor in town. Mother tried so hard and was depressed most of the time from the rejection that she suffered. I

sometime wondered who was more

mentally ill, mother or Roberto, and

there was never an answer. No wonder

Mother started seeing and talking to

dead people. Before she died, I shared

my experience that I felt that someone

was living in my house and that I was

being watched.   I never got a reaction

from her but I know she was interested

in knowing more.   I was not afraid but

finding the reason why these poor souls

decided to establish a relationship with

her kept me up at night. Mother would

always would kneel down and started

praying as she claimed that these souls,

for whatever, reason, were not able to

rest in peace and needed a prayer or

two.   I never thought that was the way

to respond to restless souls, I felt you

need to engage them and make them

part of your life.

Darkness is the absence of Light

The day my three children stepped into
Gaylord's house for the first time there
were so many different reactions.
Fernando and Max (two boys) were
intrigued with the house, bothered by
the fact that they had to now live in
substandard situations, no lights, air
condition but most important no toilets.
Adjust they did, perhaps out more of no
choice but to accept situation, they went
ahead to assist, at least for a short time,
in the repair of the house with
resignation and hope. Not so Pilar, my
daughter, she exclaimed from the first

time she set eyes on the house, this house must be "bulldozed". She remained always detached, uncomfortable and unwilling to remain in the house for any period of time. When I moved the office from downtown to the house, Pilar refused to work from the main house and instead chose the unattached garage to set up what has remained the corporate office. She refused to work on the house and refused for her children to sleep the night, where else but the master bedroom next to Gaylord's green room. For years she tried to rip off all the original wooden windows and doors only to be replaced with new metal ones.

She insisted in installing a central air

system not bothering when holes were

made in the beautiful mahogany

ceilings. She placed all kinds of

artefacts around the house to guard us

against bad spirits. Lions in front of the

office, coins and pictures inside the

office, crystals in the middle of the

house. She refused to enter the main

house for any reason whatsoever. Both

of us worked out of the garage for

several years in relative harmony while

she learned all about the business and I

introduced her to all the important

partners in the industry. She was

working in New York when the

September 11th event occurred and she

was let go of her job with the illustrious

Tiffany of New York shortly after. As a

mother I felt the duty to rescue her and

she became half owner of my company

with nothing being asked in return. I

realized that I had made a mistaken

when several years later she became

very dark and abusive, she left the office

one February day in 2015 leaving

behind only the toothbrush and tooth

paste.   She insisted that I must retire,

hand over the entire business to her and

promise never work on this industry

again. If refused to go along with her

demands I will never see her children again. This was particularly hard for me in the case of Joaquin, my dearest grandson, the first grandson, with whom I had the most loving relationship ever. I will spend long hours with Joaquin teaching all I knew and protecting him from a very controlling father. In order to ease my pain of not seeing Joaquin I started writing letters to him, letters that were never given to him. I have decided that I will include some of them at the end of this book, as they show the desperate attempts of a grandmother to understand the reasons why she cannot be with her grandchild.

Friends and family tried unsuccessfully to reconcile us. I agreed at the end, to all of Pilar's demands in order to retain the relationship with my grandchildren, to give up everything, the shares, the contracts, my life work. Pilar wanted more, she wanted to complete obliteration and elimination of her mother. She never signed any papers and to this day continues to be angry and punitive towards me

Pilar was born on a good Friday at the same time that Christ died, 3:10 p.m. in Bogota, Colombia. The nuns that assisted with the 15- hour delivery were so afraid that we had a child that should

have been born at another time or

place. They refused to pierce her ears,

as it is the custom when a baby girl is

born in Latin America, afraid of the

spiritual repercussions it may have.

That Friday nine other babies were born

at around the same time. The delivery

room was a large common room where

all the mothers were delivering the

babies. There was a large pail of hot

water in the middle where the babies

were bathed all at the same time.

Babies were never tagged, instead they

were taken from their mother and

dumped in the pail of water, hoping that

their mothers would remember what they looked like. I kept an eye on the baby as much as she could and was never sure it was my child when the baby was delivered to her side fully clothes and combed. Was this my child? They all looked similar. She was a different child from day 1. Never slept, kept her big eyes pierced on Me and would cry whenever she was picked up. After many weeks of sleepless nights the doctor prescribed a bit of alcohol to relax the child. At night, I would give a tiny amount of whiskey that enable Pilar to fall at sleep for at least 4 hours. This went on for months until she acquired the habit of sleeping. However, there had to be complete silence, even the most minute noise would wake her up and that was the end of the sleep. When she was a year old she was an abusive and temperamental child. Mothers of other children refused to have their children play with her as Pilar will scratch their faces, bite their legs and pushed them constantly to the floor. Pilar also would find the way to elope after taking all her clothes off sometimes walking in 10-degree temperature and knee-high snow. Many considered her behavior strange. At this time a movie had revolutionized movie goers because of the believable script. The name of the movie was "Rosemary Baby" and described how the devil procreated his child using a normal mother. Some in my family will call Pilar a Rosemary baby. Her brothers grew up afraid of her as she forced them to do her will or face the consequences. Max, the middle child, was in the worst situation. He was mistreated and abused. Fernando, the youngest son, was lucky as she pretended that he was her own child and demanding strict obedience she never physically abuse him the way she did with Max.

Hoping that our move to Australia will change Pilar in many ways was never to happen. In Australia Pilar dressed as a "punk" black leather and all and waited until everyone was at sleep to sneak through a window and enjoy a night out with friends. Her behavior was so bizarre that I started to believe that she was indeed not my child and wonder where my sweet little girl would be. Pilar found it difficult to stay in a relationship. Went through 2 marriages that ended shortly in divorce and a lot of blood from the physical attacks. Several times she gave up pets she had claimed to love very much without any guilt or remorse. Perhaps Pilar was incapable

of love and loyalty. Perhaps that was

the reason Gaylord rejected her and

vice/versa. Perhaps that was the

reason why Pilar wanted to destroy the

house and refused to be in it for more

than a few minutes. I always wanted to

have a big harmonious family. A family

that would get together once in a while

and enjoy each other. That the cousins

could play together the way I did with

my cousins when growing up. I have

often asked Gaylord why this is

happening and if I could have done

something to avoid it. They grew up

very closed, most of the time far away

from the rest of the family. They

depended on each other for everything.

What set them apart, what I did while

bring her up to create this anger towards

me.   Perhaps the fact that mental

illness has always been present in the

family or that now Pilar was

experiencing middle-age a time when

you take stock of what you have done in

life by yourself and that time was

running out to make a big impact on life.

Mental illness existed in the family, both

families. Pilar's grandmother died in a

nursing home after refusing to accept

that her husband had abandoned her

and refusing to hold any relationship

with her children if they dare talk to him.

She attempted suicide once and would

go on in spurs of delusions all to often.

As I had done before, I decided to go up

to the room where I had seen Gaylord

for the first time. Only in that room I felt

secure and calm. Perhaps it was fresh

ocean breeze that brought me back to

the days in Cuba where I escaped in my

little wooden boat. Looking for answers

as to the behavior of my only daughter I

started talking to myself. After a few

minutes I felt his presence and then his

dark rimmed glasses appeared as in the

first day but this time it was different. I

heard his voice first softly and then

stronger and more talkative. The

subject of children was important to him.

He had children and he was in a good

position to give advice. He went on to

talk about the two other children,

Fernando and Max. Fernando had set

up an office in Gaylord's room. I asked

Fernando often if he had felt any

strange movement in the room and he

always said no. I took that to be the

Gaylord had approved him to share his

space. Gaylord spoke of Fernando's

good nature and inquisitive mind that he

inherited from his father. In many ways

Fernando was very closed to his father and tried to imitate him. Growing up Fernando watched his father disregard and disrespect for his mother. That is why sometimes he acts in contempt for you. You once said Fernando will disappoint you, Gaylord said to my amazement. How right you are, he continued. My advice, said Gaylord, is to stop trying to buy love and respect. This makes things worst, he added. Remember you cannot change Fernando but you can change yourself. Try to put distance between both of you. I know it is difficult, but it is the only way you are going to gain his respect.

Refrain from your generous impulses.

Assert your role as a mother, remind

him that you gave him life. He reflected

for a moment and then he said, I gave

the same advice to my daughter when

she was raising her children, and it

worked. Much harm is done to the

children when parents always say Yes

to their children. Disrespect grows as

well as ingratitude and when one day

you say No, they feel you are punishing

them and they do not know why. But

Max is different because he never saw

his father as his model. In all the

photographs that I have seen around

this room, he always clung to you for

love and protection. His father constant rejection, because he was not academically up to his standards, created distance between Max and his father. In this same room, Gaylord recalled, Max and his father had a heated discussion because of his poor grades and lack of initiative. I remembered him saying to Max that he will never amount to anything. And look at him now, Gaylord said with a hint of pride, he is the most successful child of yours and he accomplished this on his own. Yes, trust Max to love and respect you. He will never disappoint you Gaylord said and disappeared.

The loss of Innocence

Where the desire to become the people's commissioner I will never know. The fact that I believed that I could bring justice and welfare to people by going into politics was the wrong assumption. I have been so involved with volunteer work and realized so much could be done if politicians truly represented the interests of those that elected them. One day in the summer of 1991 I threw my hat in the Dade County commission rate that had never had a Hispanic in their ranks. Forget that this was a very coveted seat as the

County had budgets larger than most small countries. Much was at stake, raising funds became my one priority and I was successful in raising over $1 million for a small district where only 17,000 people voted. Running for office can change your behavior and the way people look at you. Afraid that I would win at the end, most people were very condescending to me and my staff. I was so naïve about so many things, I really believed that if you ran a good race, centering on community issues and you had the experience of having worked at the community on many issues, you should win. I was not prepared for the negative campaign,

personal attacks, ballots fraud, lobbyist

demands, and the fickleness of most

voters. On top of all that, I decided,

again through naivety, to invite a major

newspaper reporter into my campaign.

The invitation included being with me 12

hours a day, seven days a week,

watching every move I made, every

interview or meeting I held and every

check that was received. Under the

promise that none of the findings were

going to be made public, I accepted.

For six months my campaign became

an open book. We received the

endorsement of every newspaper,

community organization, political group and most radio stations. My mother always accompanied me to every event taking a plate of goodies to share with the audience. The campaign went on for two years after a judge stopped the first ballots and demanded that the County elections would now be done by elaborate designed districts. The purpose, to enable more minority to win a seat. I won the county wide election but lost miserably in the district one. My opponent launched a campaign of misinformation and lies, claiming that I was a communist and against the Jewish Community. At the end, the only community that did not vote for me was

my own—full of fear that they will have

to deal with a communist, they voted for

my non-Hispanic opponent. A true

indictment of my own. All this was

known to the newspaper but they

refused to publish all these

Machiavellian maneuvers until the

election was over. A week later after

losing the election, two entire

magazines were dedicated to my

election, the stolen ballots, the negative

campaign, the misinformation, the

purchasing of votes and then more.

When I returned to my job at the

County, I was terminated immediately

under orders of the individual that won the election. One redeeming quality, for those who wanted to hear it, was that the myth that we had a representative democracy was just that, a myth.   That night when all was over, I came home in defeat, I could not stop crying. To think that I had fought so hard and that I had lost an election for something that I was not.   My family had left and it was past midnight. Some strange force pulled me up the stairs and without realizing it I was in the green room, crying uncontrollably when the window blew open. It was a cool windy April night and I was so distressed that I did not even looked up. When I did, after a few minutes, I saw this cloud in front of the window. I wiped my tears in disbelief, and then I saw these black trimmed glasses. I focused my eyes again and I could clearly see this round face man, with white bushy hair smiling at me. I just did not know what to do, stay or run, I remember my mother and her wise words about how to deal with the unknown. I did not know his name nor did he introduce himself. He just started talking to me in a soft sweat voice. Surprisingly he was aware of all that had happened to me that day.   Tears did not allow me to see him clearly this first time. Later I always saw him in the midst of a fog, but I heard his voice loud and clear, stronger every time and his dark black trimmed glasses what the first indication that he was there.

He started the conversation like this "Again, you ventured into something that you did not know enough about. That is the fearless attitude in you that has served you well of these years. Politics is a different animal. I once ran for office in Ohio and decided, early in the stage, that I did not have the stomach for it. But your nature is to never give up, and you did not. In every trip we take, there are lessons, some out of

mistakes, if we do not listen to those

lessons then all is lost, and we just

engaged in an event that would diminish

you. You are smart enough to realize

that there are many lessons and that

some gains were made by engaging in

this painful event. There were many

people that believed in you and what

you were about, they are still there, so

please make sure you retain that faith in

the good nature of people. Because of

the publicity you have become a model

for others so they can avoid the same

mistakes you made. Everyone knows

who you are the principles we stood by.

More importantly, as the result of the newspaper articles, great reforms to the absentee ballots have been made. Remember you are still the same individual, they did not destroy you or stopped you, all that happened is that you lost an election". With those words that will resonate in me for the rest of my life, Gaylord said good night. He was right, I later went on to do more important things and to make huge changes so others would live better.

The Face of Mortality

I am not afraid to die I just hate not to be here, I used to say to all my friends and family. It is no coincidence that I never said good-by to my closest family. Honestly, I would not know what to say to them in that moment, only that I loved them and I will never forget them. Concha died without my saying those words. My father too, too far away in Sydney Australia to make it to his funeral. The day my mother died I was in Central America and got on the first flight back home just to miss her by 15 minutes. She had come into the hospital with a minor infection, caught

pneumonia and died within days. She

was 97 years old and during the last

years of her life we became very close.

She finally accepted me as I was and

recognized that of all her children, I was

the one that loved her most. As I

strongly believe, not being a religious

person or a believer of the after-life, that

your dear ones live forever in your spirit,

your mind, every time you mention their

names, they are alive to you. I would

have never said good-by to mother, as

she lives in me today and while I am

alive.

Two weeks after mother died, they called me from the doctor's office to let me know that something distinct was growing inside me and they needed to check it out. I had never had surgery in my life, nor taken any medication. I was the poster child of my doctor that swore she had never seen someone so healthy. My brother, who suffered many health problems, used to call the bionic woman. That would come to an end on September 2018.

I devoted myself to ocean diving after mother's death. I found a soothing effect being underwater with the beautiful life that there existed, only with the numbing sound of my breathing through by tank. As soon as I came out, I looked at my phone and there it was a message from my doctor with dreadful news.

The results of the multiple tests revealed an invasive cancer, small enough to be surgically removed, but with no assurance that it would come back. My first reaction was total disbelief. Why would something like this happen to such a healthy person that had lived according to all the health rules. I kept asking why me? How does this happened, just to get an answer from my doctor "bad luck" I stated to questioning the entire health system.

From why my mother had died and why today, after so many years of research on Cancer there was no other method of dealing with it than "cut, burn and poison". Where have all the millions of dollars spent in finding a more natural way to cure this disease? There was never a good answer. They would tell me there are new research but it has not been tested and after all it will not be used for the type you have. I resented the fact that they would not explain the medical aspects of the disease as if you would not understand. One doctor told me that I was reading too many articles that I could not understand.   To make matter worst, my husband was given

four times the medicine for high blood

pressure while in the hospital and once

home he collapsed and almost died in

my living room. I decided not so say a

word to anybody. I just did not know

how to break the news to my children

and the rest of the family. I had to think.

I had to seek answers and help.

 It was in this frame of mind that I

climbed up the stairs in search of

answers. Gaylord had become my only

trusted source. A full moon lighted the

room with a breeze that was cool and

soothing I sat there for hours waiting for

him to appear. Tired of waiting I stood up to leave when I felt his presence behind me. His face somber and distressed. I asked why was he in such mood and why the wait. He asked me to sit down again. I had a daughter that I loved more than anything in this world and she loved me. She was so happy and had a beautiful family, a great husband and a love for life. One day, she called me to give me some news. She had been diagnosed with this terrible disease and did not know what to do.   I went through the same stages that you did, why her? There must be a mistake. Several days took me to accept this devastating news. I went

crazy finding help, identifying the best

doctors in the world that could cure this

once and for all of my beloved daughter.

Read all the latest articles on new

research and travel with her to distant

places to find the best alternative. She

underwent therapy that killed everything

good that was inside her. Like you, her

entire body was poisoned with

medication that would have helped the

disease but did so much damage. She

will not give up and neither would I. She

suffered the side effects with courage

and determination. Her entire little body

was burned and wasted. It was painful

to see what she had become as result of
the therapy and for what. My beautiful
daughter died six months after she
broke the news to me. I wonder now if it
would have been better to let it be and
let her enjoy the last few months of life
instead of being locked up in a hospital
away from her children and husband.
That is why it took me a long time to talk
to you. I do not have any answers for
you. You will have to endure the
uncertainty the way you have done
before with all the events in your life.
Continue to be skeptical of the health
profession, asking question of them,
resorting to alternatives not included in

the medical journal, live each day and count your blessings, but live with optimism. Do not give up and help others suffering with the same ailment. Share the news with your family, they are the ones that will support you to the end. Do not be afraid to face your own mortality because at the end we all do. With those words, Gaylord disappeared leaving a room full of suffering and hope.

China strikes again

In the Spring of 2020, the world awoke to a terrible menace, a pandemic like no other before. It started in a province of China and none knew what produced this virus much less how to cure it. The disease spread like fire, infecting and killing those most vulnerable, the elderly and those with health issues. Countries saw it at first as a farse, not taking it seriously, claiming it was only in China and nothing like that would come to our country. The delays in accepting and taking measures will end up in million of lives being lost. The world stood still when in March millions throughout the world were infected and dying. None was spare, rich, poor, young, old. For months researchers worked on a identifying the bacillus and finding a cure for the disease to no avail. Countries resorted to quarantine individuals, keeping them at home, closing schools, businesses, travel, closing frontiers, in the hope to buy time.

Weeks went by with no news about when this virus would be stop. In the meantime, China the incubator of the disease, had found a way to stop the number of infected and the number of fatalities went down as quickly as it had appeared. The rest of the world kept going around not knowing what to do and what to advice to their people. At the end of two months everyone became restless, the economic kept going down, unemployment in the US. Hit 30 million and our elected officials were not in agreement as to what to do next. This is the worst epidemic that I remembered in my life time. I am sure that others have occurred before and hoped that Gaylord had some insight on this.

I rushed to speak to him, although in the middle of the day, not knowing if he would show his face while the sun was shining brightly. The window was opened, it was hot outside but a nice breeze came in to sooth the senses. After waiting several minutes, I heard his voice, strong and decisively. He asked me to calm down, that at the end the world may be a better place to live. He started recounting his experience with the last pandemic that he lived through. It was called the Third Pandemic and started again in China, in the province of Yunnam, back in 1855. Infected rats brought the disease to the

US and Europe, traveling in steamships.

15 million people died. The pandemic

ended in 1950 through the discovery of

the bacillus by a Hong Kong doctor

called Alexander Yestin. The vaccine

was called Yestinian vaccine in his

honor. Going on at the same time, he

continued, was the great depression of

1920 that created havoc in the economy

and disrupted the lives of so many

people in this Country. And yet, I

survived. Never before had people

come together to fight these

phenomena. At the end we valued

more life and the people around us. We

became aware that together we could

fight anything and survive. There is nothing new my friend, he said in a loving voice, everything that is happening today happened before and individuals found a way out of it. This pandemic will follow the same path. The vaccine will come from China, from where it originated and the world once again will be immune to it for some time. The economy will recover and we will understand more than ever, how united we are and how we need to be together. Empathy will reign for a while until individuals go back to their selfish ways once again, forgetting all that was gained. The lesson here is to survive, be careful, don't take risks, and be

optimistic that this too will come to pass.

While hard try to enjoy these moments

where life became so simple. He quickly

disappeared leaving me in a different

state of mind and with good advice to

those around me.

We are what remains of us

This house was bought in November 1989 in a tumultuous auction and in the midst of much uncertainty. It has witnessed so many major events before we moved and then. I would like to think that I leave an indelibly mark on this house, not only physically but spiritually. Long days and nights of toil, scrapping paint, fixing windows and doors, repairing floors, building a new kitchen so I did not have to wash dishes on the sidewalk anymore. So much of me remains in this house and I wonder if the next tenant will sense my presence.

I raised my children here, celebrated
their weddings, had multitude of parties
with hundred of people at the end of the
year, baptized grandchildren.
Celebrated triumphs and defeats. Not
all brought joy some were times of
sorrow and deception. The loss of my
mother, the death of my loyal dog
Burnie, the loneliness after losing a
campaign and saying good-by to my
grandchildren Leon and Vicente when
they left for a new life far away, the
memories of Joaquin, dancing in the
living room and sleeping next to me,
feeling his heart and smelling his
breadth The day we baptized Maxi, my

beautiful grandson on the hottest day of the year and he did not mind.   These walls have seen so much and will continue to do so. Whoever comes after me will experience the same joy and sorrow that I have because this house was built for that to serve as a place of reconciliation, celebration, and gathering. A refuge from the world, where we can live in another time and another world, where we can smell the ocean and dream of a better world, one where harmony and peace reigns. The house built by Gaylord where there is never a right or a wrong. I have been so happy and so sad in this house. I will miss it.

I am alone in this house again, and realize it is time to leave, to another house where life could be simpler, where I can better care for myself. I have left this house in the hands of my son Fernando, who like me, was always in awe with its beauty and serenity. I know that he will take good care of it. That the grandchildren will always be welcome, they will always call this house home and where the spirit of me will live. Perhaps the family will finally be together again.

I had packed all my bags and was
waiting for the taxi to take me to the
airport. I could not leave without saying
good=by to Gaylord. I have never been
able to do so with all my dear family, my
mother, my Concha, my father, my
country. But I must try. He has always
been my source of strength, my
confidant, so many tears I have shed in
his presence. Once more. It was
getting dark and time was running out.
As I approached the room, I saw that
the window was closed and the room
was in complete darkness. There was
no breeze this hot afternoon of July. I
called his name but he did not answer. I

stood there for the longest time but he

never appeared. Was he real I asked

myself, perhaps I dreamed all this,

maybe he never existed   As I walked

towards the French doors, I stepped on

something, it was hard to see, below my

feet where a pair of black rimmed

eyeglasses.